PUFFIN BOOKS

THE WITCH'S DOG AND THE MAGIC CAKE

Frank Rodgers has written and illustrated a wide range of books for children: picture books, story books, how-to-draw books and a novel for teenagers. His work for Puffin includes the *Intergalactic Kitchen* series and the picture books *The Bunk-Bed Bus* and *The Pirate and the Pig*, as well as the other highly popular *Witch's Dog* titles. He was an art teacher for a number of years before becoming an author and illustrator. He lives in Glasgow with his wife and two children.

Frank Rodgers
The Witch's Dog and the Magic Cake

PUFFIN BOOKS

PUFFIN BOOKS

Published by the Penguin Group
Penguin Books Ltd, 80 Strand, London WC2R 0RL, England
Penguin Putnam Inc., 375 Hudson Street, New York, New York 10014, USA
Penguin Books Australia Ltd, 250 Camberwell Road, Camberwell, Victoria 3124, Australia
Penguin Books Canada Ltd, 10 Alcorn Avenue, Toronto, Ontario, Canada M4V 3B2
Penguin Books India (P) Ltd, 11 Community Centre, Panchsheel Park, New Delhi – 110 017, India
Penguin Books (NZ) Ltd, Cnr Rosedale and Airborne Roads, Albany, Auckland, New Zealand
Penguin Books (South Africa) (Pty) Ltd, 24 Sturdee Avenue, Rosebank 2196, South Africa

Penguin Books Ltd, Registered Offices: 80 Strand, London WC2R 0RL, England

www.penguin.com

First published 1999
9 10

Copyright © Frank Rodgers, 1999
All rights reserved

The moral right of the author/illustrator has been asserted

Printed in China by Midas Printing Ltd

British Library Cataloguing in Publication Data
A CIP catalogue record for this book is available from the British Library

ISBN-13 : 978-0-14038-468-0
ISBN-10 : 0-14038-468-5

W ilf, the witch's dog, had been
out for a walk.

"Hello, Wilf," said Weenie.

"I've just baked a cake for my
Auntie Flo who lives in the jungle."

(Weenie had turned her aunt
into a gorilla by mistake ...
but her aunt loved being a gorilla!)

"This cake is for
her birthday,"
she said.

The cake smelt delicious.

"Did you use magic to bake it, Weenie?" asked Wilf.

"Certainly not," said Weenie. "I never use magic to bake."

"Do you think I could bake a cake?" said Wilf.

"Of course!" replied Weenie. "I'll show you how."

5

Weenie showed Wilf how to mix the sugar, butter, eggs and flour.

But Wilf's cake mixture
was a bit
lumpy ...

and very sticky!

He got more on
himself than he
got in the tin!

Weenie put the cake in the oven ...

But when it came out
it was flat.

"It didn't rise," groaned Wilf.

"Never mind," said
Weenie. "Better
luck next time."

Weenie packed her cake into her rucksack and got on to her broomstick.

"Time for me to visit Auntie Flo now," she said. "I won't be long. Bye!"

ZOOM

She shot into the sky ...

... just as Wilf's friends – Bertie,
Harry and Streaky – arrived.

"Mmm,
there's a nice
smell in the
kitchen,"
they said.

"It's coming from this funny flat
cake," said Bertie.

12

"I made it," said Wilf. "And flat or not, I'm sure it will taste nice."

He fetched some lemonade.

"So let's have a picnic in the garden," he said.

They had just sat down on the
grass when Sly Cat and Tricky
Toad looked over the gate.

(They were jealous of Wilf because
he was top of the class at the
School of Spells.)

"That cake looks a bit small and flat," sneered Sly. He winked at Tricky. "I bet *we* can make it rise!" he said.

Sly and Tricky pointed their fingers and cast a spell.

FLASH!

The cake started to rise ...

into the air!

"We told you we could do it,
Wilf!" cried Sly and Tricky, and
they left, snorting with laughter.

Wilf and his friends stared.
The cake was getting bigger …

and bigger!

Suddenly it floated across the
grass . . .

and knocked over the gate.

The cake
sailed down
the lane and
knocked
over a
lamp post.

Wilf,
Bertie,
Harry and
Streaky
chased
after it ...

but the magic cake rose into
the sky.

"Oh no!" cried Wilf. "It might
bump into a plane!"

"Use your magic,
Wilf!" cried Bertie.
"Bring it back."

Wilf sent out a return-ticket spell.

But it didn't work. Sly and Tricky's
magic was too strong.

The cake flew on.

"What now?" yelped Harry.

"That thing is out of control!" gasped Streaky.

"I've got an idea," cried Wilf.

He grabbed the
clothes line ...

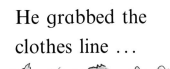

and used a flying
spell. Slowly he
lifted off the
ground ...

and flew into
the sky.

He landed on top of the
magic cake ...

and tied one
end of the
rope to it.

Then he flew
back down to
the garden,
tugging the
cake behind him.

Quickly he tied the other
end of the rope to the clothes-pole.

The cake bobbed in the sky
like a huge party balloon.

28

"Now what?" asked Bertie.

"I'll have to fetch Weenie," said
Wilf. "She'll know what to do."

"But how will you get to the jungle without a broomstick?" asked Harry. "It's a long way!"

"I'll make a broomstick," said Wilf.

"Come on. Give me a hand."

He and his friends picked up lots of
fallen twigs ...

and Wilf tied them
to a long branch.

"All I have to
do is make
it magic," said
Wilf.

He propped the broomstick
against the front door.

Then, shutting his eyes, he cast
a spell.

The broomstick fell apart.

Wilf groaned.
"Now what will
I do?" he said.

"You can fly on me," said
a voice.

"Who said that?" chorused Harry,
Bertie and Streaky.

"I did," said
Weenie's door.
It waved its
handle at Wilf.

"You missed the broomstick
and made me magic instead!"

36

The door
floated down
the steps.

"Hop on, Wilf," it said.
"We're off to the jungle!"

Wilf climbed aboard.

"I'll be back as soon as I can,"
he said to his friends, and ...

ZOOM

the door
shot into
the air.

It raced through the sky ...

and out over the sea.

In no time at all Wilf saw
the jungle down below.

The door swooped down and
flew over the treetops.

"How will we ever find Weenie?"
said Wilf. "It's like looking for a
needle in a haystack!"

"Perhaps we should ask someone,"
said the door.

Suddenly Wilf gasped and
pointed. "Look!" he cried.

"A baby monkey has fallen
out of a tree!

"Quick, door!"
he yelled.
"Down ...
fast!"

"Hold on!" it cried. "Here we go!"

The door
streaked
downwards.

43

Wilf caught the
baby monkey
just in time.

"Oh, thank you!" cried its mother.
"How can I ever repay you?"

Wilf thought.
"Do you know
a gorilla
called Flo?"
he asked.

"Of course!" she said. "I know
all the gorillas ...

she's just over
there, through
the trees."

Weenie and Flo had just
finished off Flo's birthday
cake when Wilf arrived.

They were surprised to see him.

Quickly, Wilf told Weenie
what had happened.

Weenie got on
to her broomstick.

"See you soon, Auntie Flo,"
she called.

"Let's go, Wilf!"

ZOOM!

Wilf and
Weenie shot
into the sky
and headed
home.

At Weenie's house, Sly and Tricky
had come back … and were
up to more mischief.

They put a spell on the clothes
line and made it vanish!

"Oh no! The cake is loose!"
cried Streaky.

"It's heading
for that plane!"
gasped Bertie.

"Help!" cried Harry.

The pilot stared.

"It's a UFO!" he cried.

"We're going to crash!"

Just then Wilf and
Weenie arrived.

53

Weenie cast a spell on the cake and down it went ...

in a hundred pieces.

"Hooray!"
yelled Bertie,
Harry and
Streaky.

Sly and Tricky
looked up ...
too late!

The cake shower dropped on top
of them.

"Serves them right," said Weenie
as she and Wilf landed.

"We always thought they'd come
to a sticky end," laughed Wilf's
friends.

Sly and Tricky
slunk off to
have a bath.

57

Wilf thanked
the magic
door ...

and everyone
went into the
kitchen.

"We still haven't had our
picnic," said Wilf.

So he baked
another cake ...

and this time it was perfect!
"If at first you don't succeed ..."
grinned Wilf.

Weenie, Harry, Bertie and Streaky
didn't reply.

Their mouths were too full
of Wilf's delicious cake!